SHOE FOR MY PONY

BY MARGARET FRISKEY

Pictures by
JEAN MOREY

 CHILDRENS PRESS, Chicago

Sometimes I wear no shoes.
I run through the grass in my bare feet.

But I have shoes. I have high shoes,
low shoes, and walking-through-the-town
shoes.

I have boots for walking in the rain.

And cowboy boots for riding my pony.

My pony has shoes, too. Because he
walks on hard roads, he wears horseshoes.
They protect his feet. But pony has
lost one shoe. I cannot ride him.

Pony needs a new shoe, a bright shoe,
a nail-it-on-tight shoe. But where will
I find it?

Other animals don't need shoes. Little
duck has no shoes. His feet are webbed
for swimming.

Little lamb has no shoes. He has hard hooves. They keep him from slipping when he is climbing. They protect his feet, too.

The gentle cow has no shoes. She has hooves just like little lamb.

Little kitten has no shoes. He has
paws with soft pads for tiptoeing. His
paws have claws. He can push his
claws out when he wants to catch
a mouse or climb a tree.

Rabbit has no shoes. He has paws. He can dig holes with his front feet. He can thump and jump with his strong back feet.

Pony is limping. I must walk and lead
him. "I will ask the wise owl, Pony.
Maybe he will tell me where I can
find you a new shoe, a bright shoe, a
nail-it-on-tight shoe."

But the owl did not answer. He clung to his branch with his long, sharp claws. All he said was, "Whooo? Whooo?"

I asked the hens. But they didn't answer. They just clucked and scratched the ground with their claws.

I asked the squirrels. But they didn't
hear me. They were too busy holding
nuts in their front paws and jumping
from branch to branch.

Then I met a clown with shoes as
big as paddles. I asked him.

"Ho," he said. "Your pony needs
a shoe. Go across the bridge and into
the town. Turn to the right and look
for a tall chestnut tree."

Pony and I crossed the bridge. We
turned to the right and saw the
chestnut tree.

And there we found the blacksmith.

"Can you make a shoe for my pony?"
I asked.

"Of course," he said. "I will make
your pony a horseshoe. Bring him in.
Bring him in."

Soon the blacksmith made a new shoe,
a bright shoe, a nail-it-on-tight shoe.
He put it on my pony.

Now pony isn't limping. I can ride
him. And away I went. Riding clippity,
clop. Clippity, clippity, clippity, clop.